Christmas 1996

To Sarah

From Aunt Regina

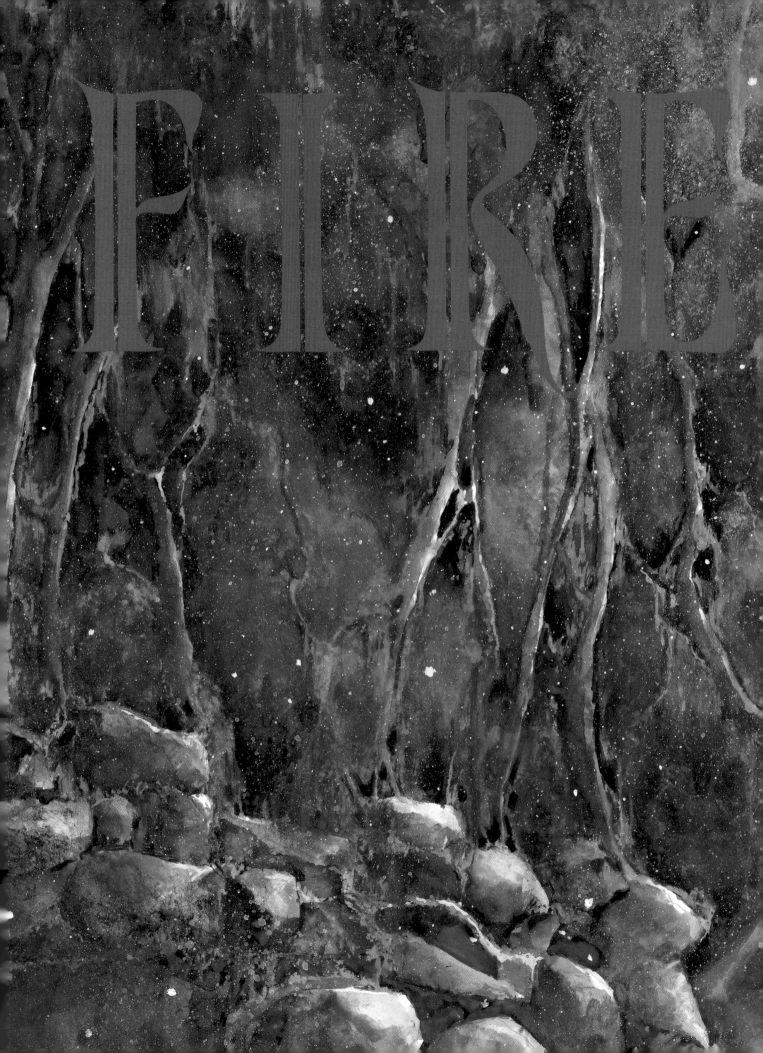

# BIRD

ADAPTED AND
ILLUSTRATED BY
**_Rachel
Isadora_**

G. P. PUTNAM'S SONS · NEW YORK

Copyright © 1994 by Rachel Isadora
All rights reserved. This book, or parts
thereof, may not be reproduced in any form
without permission in writing from the publisher.
G. P. Putnam's Sons, a division of The Putnam & Grosset
Group, 200 Madison Avenue, New York, NY 10016.
G. P. Putnam's Sons, Reg. U.S. Pat. & Tm. Off.
Published simultaneously in Canada.
Printed in Hong Kong by South China Printing Co. (1988) Ltd.
Book designed by Nanette Stevenson. Calligraphy by Dave Gatti.
Text set in Garamond Antiqua.

Library of Congress Cataloging-in-Publication Data
Isadora, Rachel. Firebird/retold by Rachel Isadora.  p.  cm. Summary: A simple
retelling of the Russian tale in which Prince Ivan encounters the magical Firebird
who helps him defeat the evil Katschei and rescue a princess. [1. Fairy tales.
2. Folklore—Russia.] I. Title. PZ8.I84Fi 1994 398.2—dc20 [E]93-1253 CIP AC.
ISBN 0-399-22510-2 10 9 8 7 6 5 4 3 2 1 First Impression

*For Gillian and Nicholas*

*Long ago in a distant land* there lived a prince named Ivan. His kingdom bordered a dark, forbidding forest. Ever since he was a boy, Ivan had heard stories about a tree of unsurpassed beauty hidden deep within the forest. It was said that magical, golden fruit grew from its branches, but whoever had gone to find this tree never returned. Seasons passed.

The snowy blanket of winter melted to reveal a new, green growth of spring. One day Ivan, now a young man, decided to go in search of the magic tree. He entered the woods, but as he wandered deeper and deeper, the undergrowth tangled about his legs, making it difficult to go on. Soon night fell and stars appeared, twinkling through the twisted branches. Just when he was too tired to search any farther, he noticed a golden glow in the distance. Quietly, he crept towards the light.

He found himself in a glorious garden, and there, in the center, stood the magic tree bearing golden fruit.

"If only I could have just one piece of fruit," Ivan thought.

Suddenly, a flash of light streaked across the sky. It soared back and forth and landed near the magic tree. The light transformed into the most dazzling creature he had ever seen—half woman, half bird, with feathers bright as flames. A Firebird!

Prince Ivan watched her from the shadows. Then he leapt forward and captured her in his arms. Terrified, the Firebird struggled to break free. Turning and twisting, she beat her wings frantically against her captor.

"This wild creature was meant to be free," he thought to himself. Gently, Ivan released his grasp. "Fly away," he whispered.

Instantly, the Firebird flew up into the air. Ivan bowed in respect and bade the Firebird farewell. But the Firebird, grateful for Ivan's kindness, removed a brilliant red feather from her tail and gave it to him.

"This feather is a magic charm. You need only wave it in time of need and I will come to you," she said. And with that she vanished into the night.

While Ivan stood motionless, he heard the sound of approaching voices. Quickly, he hid behind a bush. Ten beautiful maidens appeared, singing a haunting melody. Entranced by their beauty, Ivan stepped from his hiding place to greet them, but they drew back, frightened.

"I mean you no harm," Ivan said quietly.

The most beautiful maiden stepped forward.

"Who are you?" Ivan asked.

"We are princesses, who came here to find the magic tree, and were taken prisoner by the evil sorcerer, Katschei. This is his garden and his magic tree. Everything here belongs to him, even us. We can never escape."

Touched by the princess's story, Ivan reached out to her. The maidens danced and sang songs of joy. For that moment they seemed so happy, and Ivan was determined to save them all.

Just then, the sky darkened and a crash of thunder boomed overhead.

"Katschei!" cried the princesses fearfully. The beautiful princess gave Ivan a parting kiss and fled with her friends into the forest. Then the whole earth began to tremble and the ground opened to reveal the most terrifying sight of all. Katschei! And with him were the most hideous of monsters.

Katschei signaled his monsters to attack. From all sides, they lashed out at Ivan, and he knew he would soon be overpowered.

Then Ivan remembered the red feather. Exhausted, he managed to pull it from his pocket and wave it in the air. Suddenly, a brilliant light appeared. The Firebird had returned!

She quickly handed Ivan a golden sword, then swirled and circled in the air, hypnotizing the monsters. Ivan lunged at Katschei and killed him.

The princess ran to Ivan and together they bowed in gratitude before the Firebird. As the first rays of morning glistened through the forest, the Firebird rose in the air and flew away into the mist.

Prince Ivan and the princess returned to his kingdom and were married. Often in the evenings, just as the sun began to set, Prince Ivan would walk alone to the edge of the forest and remember....